ILLUSTRATED

Stories for GIRLS

Brown Watson

ENGLAND

CONTENTS

WHERE IS TINY?

Princess Fay loved her cat, Tiny. Tiny had been a present on her last birthday. 'So, what do you want this year?' asked the queen.

'I want to have Tiny with me all the time,' said Princess Fay.

'That is not easy,' said the queen. 'We must see what we can do!'

Next day, the princess called her cat. 'Tiny! Tiny, where are you?'

But Tiny did not appear until tea-time. She looked very pleased with herself.

'Tiny!' cried Princess Fay. 'Oh, Tiny, do not run off again!'

But Tiny was away for most of the next day and the day after. Princess Fay was nearly in tears. 'Oh, Tiny!' she cried. 'Where have you been?' But Tiny just looked pleased with herself. Next day, Princess Fay got up early. 'My birthday!' she cried. 'Now, where is Tiny? Tiny!'

Then, as Princess Fay started searching, she saw the queen in the rose garden.

 She was sitting at an easel with her painting things. And there beside her was Tiny! 'I have finished my painting!' smiled the queen. 'Come and see!'

Princess Fay looked. It was a painting of Tiny!

'I shall put the painting in a frame,' said the queen. 'So you CAN have Tiny with you all the time, just as you wanted. Happy birthday, Fay!'

Princess Fay was so happy, she had nothing to say. And, Tiny? She looked pleased with herself!

DOLLY'S THREE WISHES

Fairy liked being with all the toys.

'I did not like being with the Christmas decorations!' she told Dolly. 'I like being here!'

'Good!' said Dolly. 'Is that really a magic wand in your hand?'

'Yes!' smiled Fairy. 'I can grant three wishes, just by waving it! Make a wish, Dolly!'

'Ooh!' said Dolly. 'I DO wish I had wings like yours, Fairy!' So Fairy waved her wand – and there was Dolly with silver wings!

'Ooh!' she cried. 'Thank you very much, Fairy!'

'Look at me!' cried Dolly, as she flapped her wings and flew and fluttered around. 'Look at my wings!'

The toys smiled. Dolly did look very funny!

'You will need to rest soon,' said Blue Rabbit. 'You look tired!'

Dolly WAS tired. But when she sat in a chair, her wings dug into her back. She tried to lie down. But her wings got in the way.

Then she tried to rest on a stool.

But she kept falling off! Dolly was in tears.

'Oh, dear!' said Fairy. 'Poor Dolly! You do not like your wings, do you?'

'No,' sobbed Dolly. 'Fairy, can I wish to be just the way I was?'

So Fairy waved her magic wand – and the wings had gone.

'Thank you, Fairy!' said Dolly. 'I am myself again!'

'One more wish, Dolly!' said Fairy. 'What is it to be?'

'I wish for us all to be happy,' said Dolly. 'Just as we are!'

DOZY DORMOUSE!

Dozy Dormouse was fast asleep. 'Dozy Dormouse,' said Squirrel, 'is asleep AGAIN!'

'Quack!' went Duck. 'Sleep is no use at all!' 'So much to do, instead of sleeping!' said Rabbit. Dozy slept until the next day. Then, as soon as he woke up, he began running about, picking up ears of corn and nuts and berries! Next, he dug a hole, deep in the ground!

'Dozy IS busy!' said Rabbit.

'Now, he is eating without stopping!' said Squirrel. 'He is hungry after all that work!' Then, after Dozy had eaten all the food, he crawled into his hole and curled up into a ball.

'Well!' sniffed Rabbit. 'Dozy is going to sleep again!'

'Sleep is no use!' said Squirrel.

'You do not think so?' came the deep voice of Stag. 'See the falling leaves! Feel the cold wind! Winter is coming!'

'Winter!' quacked Duck. 'My pond will be frozen!'

'We will need to search for food!' said Squirrel.

'And try to keep warm!' said Rabbit with a shiver.

'But Dozy will sleep the winter away, until the warm weather comes,' said Stag.

They looked into the hole, where Dozy was already fast asleep.

'So, sleep is useful after all,' said Rabbit. 'See you in the spring, Dozy Dormouse!'

HELLO, HOBBY-HORSE!

Hobby-Horse stood in the broom cupboard. He was a fine hobby-horse with knots all along his mane, reins and a harness with yellow bells. But, he was lonely. 'Nobody even knows I am here anymore,' he told himself.

But, one day, the door was pulled open. 'Hey! Nita!' said a voice he had never heard before. 'A Hobby-Horse! He must have been here before we came! You can ride him in the town parade on Sunday!'

'He is not a real horse, Max,' came a second voice. 'You know that…'

'But you can go where you like on Hobby-Horse!' said Max. 'He will be better than a real horse!'

Hobby-Horse did not know about that. 'A real horse can trot and gallop,' he said to himself. 'I can only move with someone pushing me along on my wheels.'

But on Sunday, Nita took him into the street. Then she sat across his back, pushing him along with her feet, so that his wheels went round.

'Money for the animal shelter, please!' she cried, holding out a bucket. In and out among the crowds they went, with everyone wanting to give money and to get to know Hobby-Horse!

'And I can get around on MY hobby-horse!' cried Max. 'Look!' Nita looked. And Hobby-Horse looked. Max was on a hobby-horse with black knots along his mane!

'Another hobby-horse!' said Hobby-Horse. 'I will never be lonely again!' And he never was.

HERE COMES JESSIE!

All the animals at the big safari park knew Jessie the Jeep! She was always busy, bringing things for them or taking Wendy, her driver, around the safari park.

One day, Wendy drove the vet to see a monkey and her baby.

'The baby is still small,' said the vet 'But she is doing well!'

'Good!' said the keeper. 'It is the first baby for that monkey!'

'Come on, Jessie!' smiled Wendy. 'You can see Baby Monkey later!'

Jessie fetched hay and blankets for the donkeys. She worked hard all day. Then Wendy got a call on her radio.

'Baby Monkey is missing!' cried the keeper. 'Have you seen her?'

'No!' said Wendy. 'I shall drive around the safari park in Jessie!'

'Good idea!' said the keeper. 'The monkey is fretting badly! And the baby needs her mother!'

They looked all over the safari park.

'It will be dark soon!' said Wendy. 'We must find her!'

'We are all worried!' said the keeper. 'Only Jessie doesn't seem upset!'

'I feel cold!' said Wendy. 'I left my jacket on the back seat!'

She reached across – and touched something furry! It was Baby Monkey, fast asleep!

'Well!' said Wendy. 'Thanks, Jessie!'

Baby Monkey liked riding in Jessie! And when she saw her baby, Mother Monkey jumped up on the jeep!

'Look at that!' said Wendy. 'ALL the animals DO know Jessie the Jeep!'

21

FLUFFY CAT'S LUCKY CHARM

One day, Fluffy Cat found something on the floor. It was round and red, with a hole in the middle. 'What a pretty bead!' she said. 'It can be my lucky charm!'

Fluffy Cat went to pick the bead up, but it rolled into a mouse hole. She reached inside, and – ouch! – she scraped her paw! It did hurt!

'Never mind!' she said. 'I still have my lucky charm!'

But even as Fluffy Cat spoke, the bead slipped from her paw.

23

'Never mind! said Fluffy Cat. 'I can soon pick it up!'

She bent down, and – BUMP! – she bumped her head on the windowsill! It did hurt!

'Never mind,' she said. 'I still have my lucky charm!'

She held the bead tightly. But it still slipped from her paw and rolled under a pile of puzzles!

'Never mind,' said Fluffy Cat. 'I can soon pick it up!'

She bent down, and – CRASH! – down fell the puzzles!

'Fluffy Cat!' cried Dolly. 'What ARE you doing?'

'Picking up my lucky charm!' said Fluffy Cat. 'But this red bead has not been very lucky so far! Ooh, my poor head! My sore paw!'

'Red bead?' said Dolly. 'It is the wheel that the wooden horse lost! We have all been looking for it!'

'Never mind, Fluffy Cat!' smiled Robot. 'The little wheel may not have been lucky for you, but it was lucky for the wooden horse that you found it!'

BUZZ, BUZZ, BUSY BEES!

'Silly bees!' said Farmer. 'There is no pollen inside the flowers on these tiles on my kitchen wall!' He opened a window. 'Buzz off! Find real flowers!'

'Buzz! Buzz-z-z!' went the bees.

'These bees!' said Hector Horse. 'As they buzz around collecting pollen to make honey, they help plants to make new plants. They want pollen from the flowers on your hat, Donny Donkey!'

'But my flowers are plastic!' said Donny. 'Buzz off, bees!'

Clara Cow was eating grass in the meadow. 'These bees!' she mooed. 'They are all buzzing around these lovely buttercups!' 'They want pollen so that they can make honey!' said Hector.

'And as bees collect pollen, they help plants to make new plants,' said Donny. 'Look! They are going to the vegetable patch! Which flowers will they find there?'

'Let us go and see!' said Hector. Peas, tomatoes and cabbages all grew in the vegetable patch.

The bees did not bother with those! They buzzed busily around the orange flowers of the runner beans and the yellow flowers of the marrows! 'Buzz-buzzzz!'

'See these bees!' said Donny. 'They are collecting pollen to make honey for the farmer!'

'And they are helping plants to make new plants,' said Hector again. 'That means new crops of winter feed for us!'

'What busy bees!' mooed Clara.

'Buzz-buzz-z-z!' went the bees.

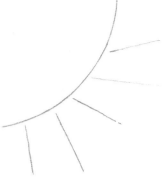

WHATEVER THE WEATHER

Jan had a little weather house. If the weather was wet, Rainy-Day Man came out. If it was fine, he went inside and out came Sunshine Doll. It began to rain. Out came Rainy-Day Man. Then, the sun came out. Rainy-Day Man went inside the weather house, and Sunshine Doll came out. Just for a moment, Rainy-Day Man and Sunshine Doll saw each other. They wished they were able to spend some time together.

It started to rain. So, Sunshine Doll went in. 'See my weather house!' said Jan. 'Rainy-Day Man comes out as Sunshine Doll goes in! Then, she comes out and Rainy-Day Man goes in!'

'Rain one minute, sun the next!' said Mum. 'That is springtime!'

Just then, the weather house gave a wobble. 'It must be all this coming and going by Rainy-Day Man and Sunshine Doll!' said Mum. 'The little house is only fixed to the wall by a little peg!'

As Mum spoke, the peg snapped. CRASH! The weather house fell to the floor.

'Well,' said Mum. 'Rainy-Day Man and Sunshine Doll will not work, now.'

Jan and Mum managed to fit all the bits back together. Then Mum fixed Rainy-Day Man and Sunshine Doll by the front door.

Jan was pleased to see Rainy-Day Man and Sunshine Doll together!

'Look!' she cried. 'They are smiling at each other!' And, so they were.

AMY THE AMBULANCE

'Calling Amy the Ambulance! Susan Mills has had a fall in Hill Park. Bring her to hospital! Over!'

Jo, Amy's driver, flicked a switch on her radio. 'Amy calling! We are on our way! Over and out!'

Susan was crying. 'My arm hurts! And my doll is broken!'

'It is her arm that is broken!' said Nurse Paula. 'Amy the Ambulance will take you both to hospital!'

'I do not want to go to hospital!' sobbed Susan.

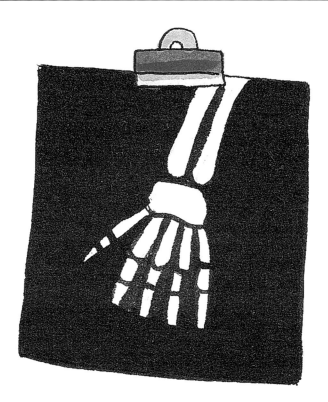

'Dina cannot go alone,' said Mum.

Susan gave a sniff. She stopped crying. 'All right,' she said.

Paula helped Susan into Amy the Ambulance. 'Dina needs a plaster on her face,' she said. 'Let us find one in Amy's first-aid box!' Susan put a plaster on Dina's face. Then she helped to bandage Dina's leg.

At the hospital, a doctor took an X-ray picture of Susan's arm. 'You have broken your arm,' he said. 'We must put it in a plaster cast. It will mend in six weeks.'

Later, Paula put Dina's broken arm in plaster, too. 'Dina's plaster cannot come off,' said Mum. 'Toys cannot mend like we can, Susan.'

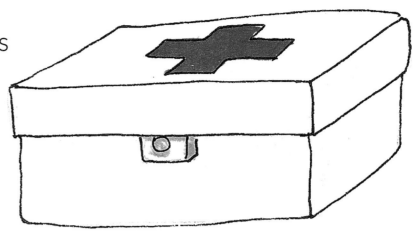

Susan stroked Dina's hair. 'I do not think she minds,' she said, 'as long as she can stay with Amy!'

'Good idea!' said Paula. 'With her big smile, her arm in a sling and a plaster on her face, she will make everyone feel better about going to hospital!'

'Yes!' said Susan. 'And Amy the Ambulance will be taking them!'

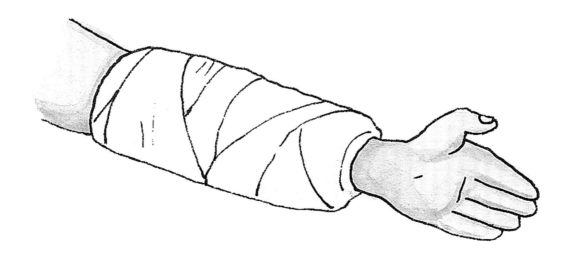

THE STAR OF THE SHOW

'We are putting on a special show!' said Pinky Pig. 'And we are going to have a special star! Will you help us, Rag Doll?'

'Ooh, yes!' said Rag Doll.

Rag Doll draped the puppet theatre with green paper. She threaded green creepers on string. She put lots of sand on the stage. She was looking forward to the special show. She might even meet the star!

She looked around at the theatre.

It seemed to shimmer, like waves in an underwater cave.

'Oh…' said Rag Doll in wonder. She touched a coloured fish. Its tail waved, making the green creepers ripple. 'It is like magic!'

Something was shining in the sand.

'A treasure chest!' breathed Rag Doll. She lifted the lid. 'Beads! A bracelet to go on my wrist! And a crown for my head!'

Rag Doll gazed all around. 'What a lovely place,' she said.

The green creepers rippled again.

'It is like a dream…'

There was another sound. It was the sound of clapping!

'What a lovely show!' said Fairy. 'All about a princess finding her crown among the treasure!'

'Princess?' gasped Rag Doll. 'Crown? Treasure?' She turned this way and that, looking around for Pinky Pig. 'But, Pinky, what about the special show?'

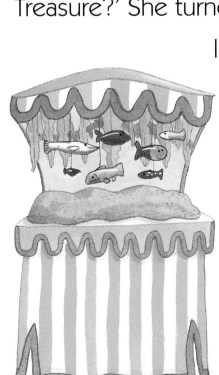

'It WAS a special show!' said Pinky. 'Because YOU were the star of the show, Rag Doll!'

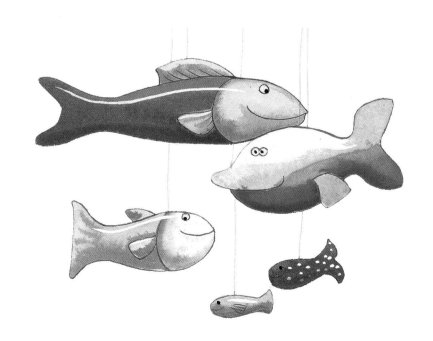

THE MUSHROOM IN THE RAIN

Ladybird was in the wood. It began to rain. He looked around for a place to shelter. There was only a tiny mushroom, so Ladybird scuttled underneath. And, it kept him dry!

A big snail came crawling by.

'I hope that snail will not come under my mushroom,' said Ladybird. 'There is no room!'

But, the snail crawled in beside Ladybird out of the rain. And, they both kept dry.

Then a butterfly came fluttering by. 'I hope that butterfly does not come under our mushroom!' said Ladybird. 'There is no room!'

But the butterfly fluttered down beside him. And, they all kept dry.

There was another flutter of wings. It was a baby owl. 'I hope that owl will not come under our mushroom,' said Ladybird. 'There is no room!' But the owl flew in under the mushroom. And Ladybird, the snail, the butterfly and the owl all kept dry.

The rain stopped. Out came the baby owl, the butterfly, the snail and Ladybird. 'We all kept dry!' he cried. 'Yet we only had a tiny mushroom!'

'Whoooo!' hooted Mother Owl. 'It WAS a tiny mushroom before the rain. Now, look!'

So, they looked. The top of the mushroom had spread out, getting bigger as the rain fell!

'So, there WAS room for us all!' said Ladybird. 'And the mushroom helped us to keep dry!'

CLARA, AT HOME AND AWAY

To Todd and Una, Clara the Caravan was a friend. With Clara being towed by the family car, they went to stay at the seaside, in camping parks, forests and woods.

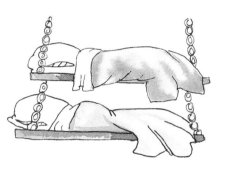

'I like going to bed in Clara's pull-down bunks!' said Todd.

'I like keeping all our toys in Clara's lockers,' said Una.

'But it will soon be time for us to go back to school,' said Todd.

'We will miss being in Clara,' said Una. They felt sad about that.

'Cheer up!' said Mum. 'Clara will be taking us to Uncle Tony's wedding this weekend!' Uncle Tony lived in an apartment block. In the grounds was a big garden. And in the garden was a marquee, like a big tent.

'This is for our wedding party!' said Uncle Tony. 'You can put Clara here!'

It was a nice wedding. But being with Clara made it even nicer.

'I DO like your caravan!' said Sally, Uncle Tony's wife. 'It must be such fun, staying inside!'

'Come and see us!' said Mum. 'Then you can stay in Clara, too!'

'Can we stay in Clara?' asked Una. 'When we go home, I mean?'

'That is a good idea!' said Mum.

So when she is not taking them on trips to the seaside, forests or camping parks, Clara is a playroom for Una and Todd, where they can invite friends. And there is always room for visitors!

'Being with Clara is as much fun at home as when we go away!' said Todd. 'She is a real friend!'

NO RUST FOR ROBOT!

The bath-toys were in the sink having lots of fun! 'Quack!' went Duck, splashing water.

'Whirr!' went the boat, chasing bubbles.

'Whee!' went Whale, flapping his flippers. 'MUST you be so noisy?' said Rag Doll. 'Robot is not welll!'

'It is a touch of rust,' said Robot. 'Rust makes me stiff and clanky.'

'Have a rest in the wendy house,' said Fairy. 'And DO be quiet, bath-toys! Just for a little while!'

'Wheee!' went Whale. 'I shall make some soapy bubbles!' But, as he reached for the soap, it shot out of his flippers and on to the floor!

BUMP! Down went Robot, slipping and sliding on the soap!

'Poor Robot!' said Fairy. 'Can you move? Can you get up?'

'I do not think so,' said Robot.

'Be careful,' said Rag Doll. 'You are lying on the soap!'

The toys tried moving Robot, first one way and then the other. But he was too heavy.

Next, they tried lifting Robot, first one way and then the other.

'Do try to move, Robot!' said Blue Rabbit. 'Just a little bit!'

'I am so stiff,' Robot began. Then he stopped. 'My rusty arm!' he cried. 'I can move it! It is not sore!'

'That arm is COVERED in dirty soap!' said Fairy. 'What a mess!'

'Wheee!' cried Whale. 'The soap got rid of the rust! Robot will not feel stiff and clanky now!'

'No!' cried Robot. 'I feel like a new robot!'

FAIRY PANSY

'How can I see a human child?' Fairy Pansy asked Fairy Moth.

'There is one at the end of our garden!' said Fairy Moth. 'Such lovely hair, tiny feet, a sweet face and a soft voice! Wait and see!'

So Fairy Pansy hid among the flowers, waiting. After a while, there came the sound of footsteps. Fairy Pansy peeped out – only to see big, flat feet with heavy boots. And the face did not look sweet at all!

'Fairies at the bottom of our garden, Meg?' came a voice. 'Huh!'

Fairy Pansy peeped out again. She still hoped to see a sweet face with long hair. But the face was round, with a snub nose and short hair.

'Mark!' came another voice. 'What are you staring at?' 'Er…' came the reply. 'For a moment, I was sure I saw…er…'

'Fairies at the bottom of our garden?' finished Meg. 'That is what I am always saying, Mark!'

Mark walked off, kicking at the grass. But Meg parted some of the flowers and looked more closely. Fairy Pansy sat among the flowers, her face in her tiny hands.

'Well!' breathed Meg. 'I SAID there were fairies at the bottom of our garden!'

Fairy Pansy took her hands away. She saw the lovely face, the long hair and the smooth skin.

'At last!' she said in her soft, tiny voice. 'I have seen a REAL human child!'

MOLE FINDS A HOME

Mole lived in a long, dark, damp
tunnel. He did not like his home!

'This is where we are safe,' said Father
Mole. 'It is fine for us!'

'It is not fine for ME!' said Mole to himself.
'I am leaving!'

He went along the tunnel. Just ahead was a hole.
Sunshine beamed down. Mole climbed and poked his
head outside. Just as he did, a spade appeared above him
and almost hit him on the head! The man digging the hole
hadn't even noticed Mole!

Mole ran under a hedge, as quickly as he could.

Then, something round and hard landed on the ground next to him.

'What a hit!' came a voice. 'Where did that cricket ball go?'

Mole ran off and escaped down a rabbit hole. He bumped right into a big rabbit!

'Out of our home,' cried the rabbit, 'You are frightening my babies!'

Poor Mole! Suddenly, he felt very lonely and tired. Then he heard a voice he knew.

59

'So there you are, Mole! Where did you go?' It was Father Mole!

'I found a lawn,' panted Mole. 'But a man didn't notice me and almost hit me on the head with a spade! Then a cricket ball just missed me, so I ran down a hole and a rabbit shouted at me!'

'And now you are just in time for dinner!' said Mother Mole.

Mole opened his mouth to speak again. Then he looked around the tunnel, sniffing its smells and feeling the soft ground. It was so good to be home!

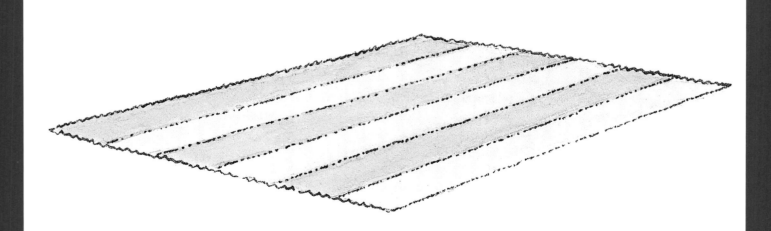

KITE AT THE SEASIDE

Kite had been to so many places! High up in the sky on his long string, he had seen green fields and wide rivers and busy roads. Best of all, Kite liked the seaside!

'I just cannot describe it!' he told the toys. 'There is so much to see at the seaside!'

'Maybe,' said Fluffy Cat. 'But none of us will ever see it!'

'What is the seaside like?' asked Clown. 'Can you tell us, Kite?'

Kite looked around.

'That tin tray!' he said. 'The sea is like that, smooth and shiny!'

'Put it on the floor!' said Clown. So that is what the toys did.

'Put some bricks on top!' said Kite. 'They can be toy boats!' So that is what the toys did.

'We need a sandy beach!' Kite went on. 'That bit of brown paper at the bottom of the cupboard! Put it on the floor!' So that is what the toys did.

Then Dolly opened her pink umbrella and put it on the beach.

'Now we need pebbles to play with!' said Kite. He looked around again. 'Those bits of jigsaw puzzle can be pebbles! Put them in a heap on the beach! Now we are all at our very own seaside!'

And so they were. Dolly and Fairy sat under the beach umbrella. Blue Rabbit and Clown sailed boats on the sea. Fluffy Cat and Rag Doll played with the pebbles. And, Kite? High up on his long string, he just liked being at the seaside!

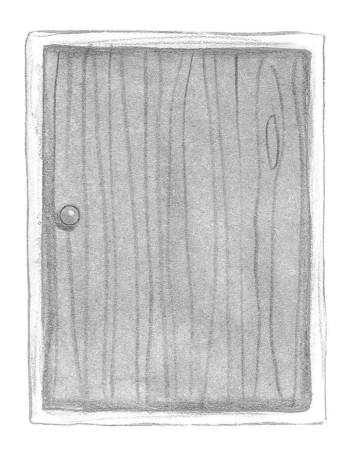

First published 2008 by Brown Watson
The Old Mill, 76 Fleckney Road
Kibworth Beauchamp
Leicestershire LE8 0HG

ISBN: 978-0-7097-1830-7

Reprinted 2009, 2010, 2011
Printed in Malaysia